CW00853037

The Ellie Adventures

STORIES & ARTWORK

BY

JONATHAN LIDDELL

ISBN 978-1-909675-995
First edition published in 2020 by Swan & Horn.

British Library Catalogue in Publication Data: a catalogue record for this book is available from the British Library.

Editing and production Maria H Carter.
Editorial assistance Sophie Hampshire.
Printed in the UK.

BOOK ONE

You Have All You Need

DEDICATED TO

the countless friends and family who have waited for this book, and those who nudged it in the right direction

Descendora is a small group of islands that could be anywhere in the world, although the landscape most closely resembles that of Scotland. This is where Ellie lives, with her Uncle Dutch and a few of her feathered and furry friends.

Table of Contents

CHAPTER 1

Fresh Air

Ellie sat at home, pencil in hand, and tried to get on with her homework.

She looked at it one way, and looked at it another.

"It's no use … I can't do it!"

"Nonsense," grunted Dutch from the stove. "Of course you can."

"No, you don't understand. I feel a bit funny," she groaned. "I can *feel* it! Sort of like …"

She gestured impatiently, searching for the right words.

Dutch looked over his shoulder. "Like ants in your tummy?"

"Like ants in *what*? Well …" Ellie paused to think. "Yes, I guess so."

Dutch looked up from his stew. It would need to sit for a bit yet before it would taste just right. Stews are like that. They need time. He popped in a bay leaf just to be sure.

"You need some fresh air, young'un," said Dutch.

"No, I need to finish my homework!"

"You need fresh air first. Go get your things."

Ellie sighed, but smiled. Uncle Dutch nagged her awfully, but he was usually right.

She ran up the stairs and grabbed her rucksack.

Paper and pencils, a scarf—just in case—and a medical kit (also just in case). Dutch was always carrying spare jumpers with that very thought.

She pulled out an old woollen jumper that had once belonged to Dutch before it had shrunk to half its size in the wash. A few alterations later and it was the cosiest one she'd ever owned.

She hopped back down the stairs to find Dutch holding out a water bottle in one hand and a thermos flask in the other.

"Just in case," he winked.

She stuffed them into the side pockets of her rucksack, all ready to go.

"One more thing, Ellie … Here."

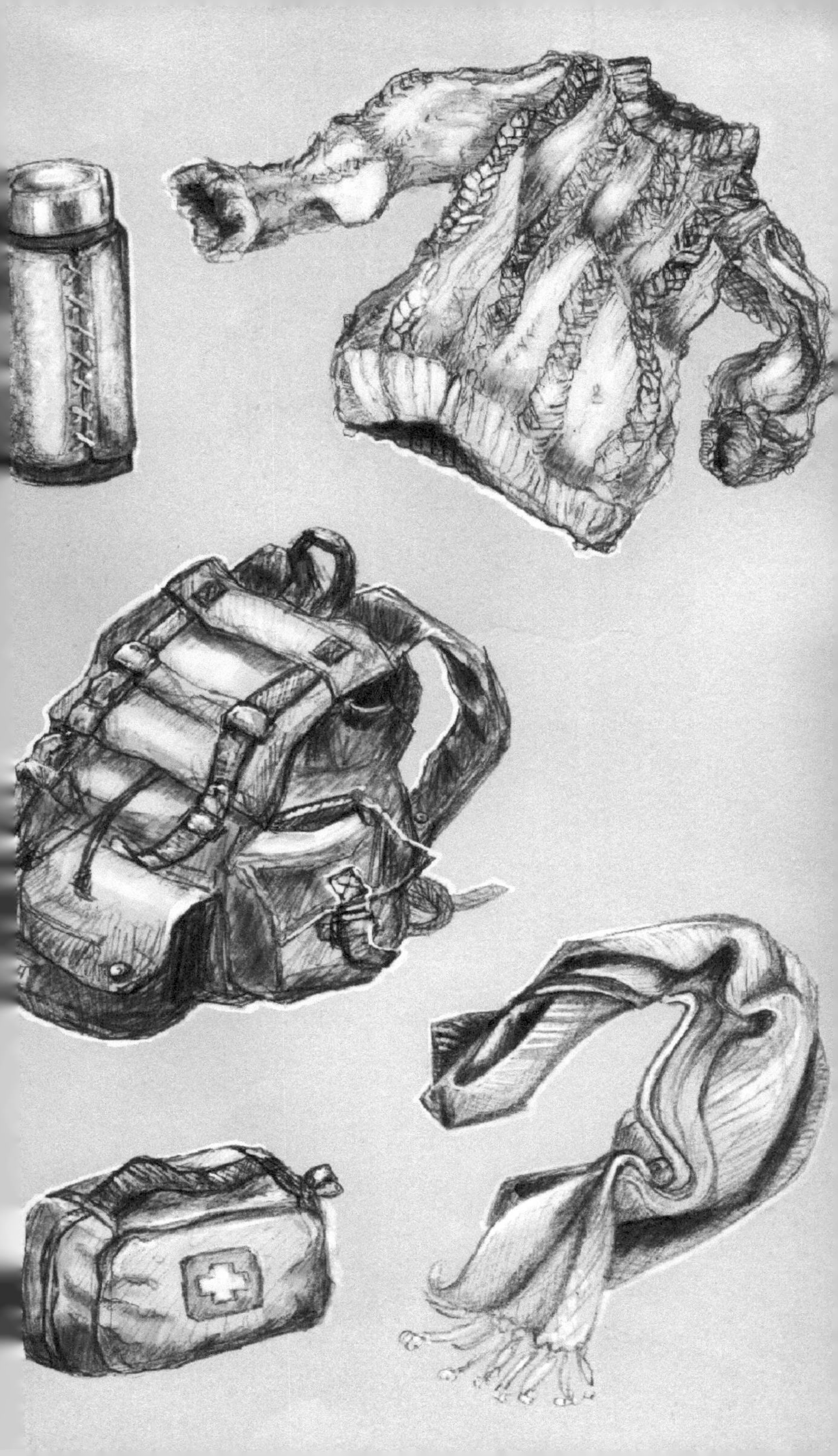

He pulled a crimson, leatherbound sketchbook out from a side drawer.

"Rose never started this one. I'm sure she'd want it put to good use."

He opened it to the first page, then, taking his fountain pen from his breast pocket, he wrote:

Dear Ellie

You have all

You Need.

D.

"Thank you, Dutch."

Her uncle rarely spoke about his wife, Rose. Or the baby.

He smiled softly, lost in thought.

Dear Ellie,
You have all
You Need.
D.

Dutch sniffed the air. "There's a cold wind blowing in from the sea. Did you remember your scarf—*just in case*?"

"I did!" Ellie headed off towards the hills. "And I'll be back before tea!" she called out with a wave.

"You'd better! This stew won't eat itself!"

But I might, he thought to himself.

"Now remember—you have all you need, Ellie!"

Dutch turned and went back to his stew-pot. *Maybe a bit more pepper …*

CHAPTER 2

Fields & Stones

Spring was shaking off the reluctant cold grip of winter. Snow still clung to the mountain tops in defiance, sparkling in the sun.

Ellie passed new lambs taking their first steps while others frolicked about, just for the fun of it.

Reaching the top of the brae, she looked out over Dutch's cabin and beyond, to the seaside town she knew so well.

She blew one long whistle, pulled down her sleeve to cover her hand …

… and waited.

With silent grace, Barn Owl appeared on her arm.

"Hello, old friend," she said softly.

Dark eyes looked up at her.

Barn Owl blinked, gave a bob of hello, and nuzzled Ellie's nose with its beak.

They set off toward the foot of the mountain, following the river as it trailed up to its birthing place amid the hidden peaks.

The pines swayed and creaked, the water played its tune against the rocks. Ellie came to a clearing and there they were—the Rose Falls.

Majestic, they towered in pink stone and crashing water. They crashed in a forever fall of white water that pooled and spiralled in dark depths before rounding a bend and winding on through rocky banks and moss-coated trees. The red bark of the pines and dark green needles framed their wonder, lost in mist-filled air.

Ellie hopped over rock and stone, wet with gentle spray. Clambering over the rocks, she got higher and higher, closer and closer to the top.

At long last, she was there.

She sat tall, looking out to sea, the wind playing in her hair.

On the horizon, the fishing boats dotted out as naught but blips. The tiny seaside town, nestled on the rocky shore, reduced to dolls' houses and toys.

Looking down from the falls, a familiar face padded in to view.

"Bear!" Ellie called with a wave.

The great Bear towered on its hind legs, ears pricked. It raised a paw and smiled the way only bears can.

Seeing lunch swimming off, Bear splashed to and fro to catch a salmon.

CHAPTER 3

The Fall

Ellie began to work once more.

I have all I need … I have all I need … she recited.

She breathed in deep, closed her eyes and tried to focus.

Clouds wisped by, pine needles swayed in the trees, and all was quiet, and at last peaceful. Ellie sipped tea from her thermos.

Bear continued to fish. Barn Owl gazed down at them both, listening—as only owls can.

The stress of working eased as Ellie kept going, writing and sketching and getting her thoughts down.

She was close to finishing, when doubt crept in from the darkness of her mind.

It's not good enough.

Uncertainty swirled in her stomach. Doubt stole away her focus.

The wind picked up, rattling the pine needles and creaking the great branches above.

Everything began to look sinister. Suddenly she was afraid and frustrated.

She packed away her things in a hurry, and pushed down dark thoughts with a building rage.

The sketchbook lay discarded at her side.

It will never be good enough.

Ellie knew she loved to draw, but what help was that in a world full of problems?

She picked up the sketchbook.

Hearing Ellie stuff her things roughly into her rucksack, Barn Owl looked down … just in time to see Ellie clamber onto a big wet rock.

She knows better than that!

Ellie yelled out as all her pain and disappointment bubbled to the surface. So much had gone wrong in such little time. None of it was fair!

She looked down at the sketchbook, teary with rage. Blotches formed on the pages as tears rolled off her cheeks.

With a final shout she flung the book away.

Silence …

Splosh! It hit the water—her Uncle's gift.

Oh no. What have I done? No, no, no!

With a fright, she turned quickly to climb back down. She must catch up with it before it was lost. She *must* catch it, she *must*, she …

… she slipped. The world stopped.

Ellie fell. Wings spread.

Cold. Wet. The wind knocked out of her.

Stupid! How stupid!

The weight of the water, now soaked into her clothes, pulled Ellie down into the depths. She was flooded with fear.

The wicked current spun her around, confusing up from down. In her panic, she grasped at wet stones that slipped from under her fingers.

More fear. Cold fear. Hot pain.

She couldn't breathe.

Oh no …

Ellie's feet struck the riverbed.

No, no! I won't sink!

She kicked up hard and broke the surface.

Gasping for air, she fought to stay above water, her hands searching for safety. They found a moss-covered stone and held tight.

She pulled herself along, against the fast flow, the depths receding to shallows.

Her body was full of bumps and bruises and she hurt as she tumbled over loose rocks with the current, searching wildly for the sketchbook in every direction.

At last! There it is!

She grasped at its spine, the pages all splayed out. Her Uncle's message to her soaked through. His words bleeding into the paper.

Ellie clutched the sodden sketchbook to her chest with one arm as she struggled toward the riverbank.

Barn Owl had swooped down to Bear before Ellie had even hit the water.

Abandoning a tasty lunch, Bear had crashed through the shallows to see Ellie struggling.

Strong jaws clamped on her rucksack to haul her from the water.

Exhausted, Ellie looked up to soft amber eyes.

"Bear? I'm alright. I'm alright. That was … daft."

It certainly was, agreed Bear, eyes full of worry.

Ellie was soaked, shivering and light-headed with fright.

I have all I need … I have all I need …

Her body groaned with many angry bruises.

"*Eugh*, that's all I need, alright! Everything hurts."

Bear hauled her up on to huge shoulders, where hot fur began to soak up the wet and cold. She clung tightly to thick fur. Her head felt woozy.

I must stay awake, she thought.

She still shivered as Bear hurried in the direction of home.

Barn Owl took flight, hovering above them, before soaring to the cabin.

CHAPTER 4

Lessons Learned

Ellie woke in her own bed, with warm toes in front of a roaring fire.

The sketchbook hung on a line, pages curled and crinkled.

I've ruined it.

Ellie hung her head, tears threatening to return.

Dutch rose from his chair.

"You're awake." He smiled, hiding his concern.

"How's the head? You gave us all quite a fright, young'un."

Ellie groaned and pulled the duvet higher, balling it in her fists.

Dutch came and sat at the foot of the bed.

"Ellie, what were you working on?"

From deep within the covers came a muffled reply.

"We had to draw ourselves with our loved ones. But the picture's wet and damaged now … and I *couldn't do it*."

There was a pause.

"*They're gone, anyway*!" she snapped sharply.

Memories caught in her chest like defensive bees around a hive.

Her eyes were hot and teary.

She surfaced from the duvet, and the pair sat in silence for a moment.

"Dutch, I'm sorry. I—I got mad. I threw it. I threw the sketchbook away."

Dutch looked at her, his fierce young niece, just as her mother had been. He hugged up the most precious thing he had in the world.

"No matter, Ellie. When it's dry it'll be as good as new. A bit crinkled, yes, but good enough. Rose used to use anything she could find to write and draw on—a napkin and pen borrowed from a reluctant waiter, a pencil stub and an old newspaper. Even my fountain pen disappeared on occasion … along with the crossword."

Dutch looked intently into his niece's eyes.

"The tools aren't important, Ellie. What is important is that you use what you have, and that you believe you can *do it …*"

"I've seen you work—*I believe* you can do it, but now it's time *you* did."

Ellie pondered this.

"I know it's been tough," he continued. "For all of us."

Ellie sat at the table, pencil in hand, the pages (now dry) spread out before her.

I have all I need …

She began to draw.

Ellie put down her pencil, placing it between the pages of the open sketchbook. She bounced up and beamed at her uncle.

"Dutch, I'm going out for some eggs! The chickens need cleaned out anyway," she called as she dashed past him, heading for the door.

"I'll serve up in a minute then. This stew will be ready when you get—" he replied to any empty space.

Dutch leaned over the table and smiled at the open pages. *That's it, Ellie.*

His eyes cast towards a framed photograph on the mantlepiece.

Thank you, Rose.

Before long, Ellie popped back with the eggs and washed her hands.

The pair sat across the table, and Dutch ladled out two bowls of steaming stew as Ellie buttered some thickly sliced bread.

"Not bad, Dutch. Not bad at all," Ellie said between mouthfuls.

Dutch chuckled and reached for second helpings.

"So, Ellie. What's next?"

She grinned and reached for her sketchbook.

THE END

Over To You

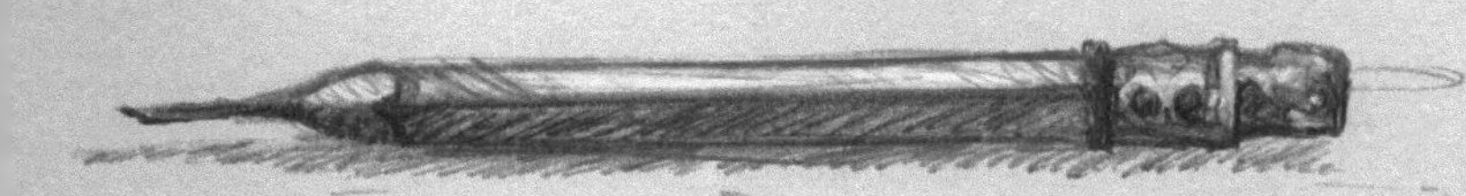

Grab a pen or a pencil …

In Chapter 1, Ellie pac

What do you pack when yo

to go on an adventure.

a journey? Where do you like to go?

In Chapter 2, Ellie
Are there things that sometime
things r

strated and gets upset.

ou? How do you go about making

o do you turn to?

So upset is Ellie in Chapter 3 t
Can you think of a time you
you d

does something she wishes she hadn't.

et and did the same? What did

e things right?

In Chapter 4, we learn

Who has given you a

tch has some advice for Ellie.

'he past? What did you learn?

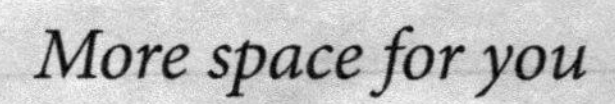
More space for you

More space for you

More space for you

More space for you

More space for you

More space for you

More space for you

More space for you

More space for you

More space for you

More space for you

More space for you

About the Author

Jonathan Liddell has had various teaching roles over the years, working closely with children of all ages who find themselves in difficult life circumstances.

He also runs creative-writing workshops.

He graduated in 2016 from the DJCAD Masters in Art, Society & Publics, and was awarded the William Sangster Phillip fund.

His stories focus on "relatable challenges and how to overcome them, nodding to the small joys in life" with humour and sensitivity, as he celebrates families and friends, and promotes the simple pleasures.

With recent funding from the Scottish Book Trust and Creative Scotland, he is actively engaging children in story-telling activities during the pandemic—a truly modern challenge.

Jonathan's illustrations draw on Scotland's landscape, wildlife, and nourishing outdoor spaces.

"My hopes for this book are that it inspires others to pick up a pencil and sketch delight back into their lives, to share that with their loved ones, and to provide a tale that points to the importance of close friends and the confidence to step forward for yourself."

@jonathan.liddell